His Dirty Secret

Book 5

Mia Black

Table of Contents

Prologue

Jayla

I busted into my condo and made sure to lock the door behind me. I was panicking. I can't believe what just happened. I needed something to drink. No. I needed to get help. What the fuck man? What the fuck!

"What is going on?" Keon was sitting on the couch, cool and collected. It looked like he didn't have a care in the world. "You are looking all types of crazy right now." I heard him, but I kept pacing the room.

"Oh my God." I repeated it a million times and started rocking back and forth. "What am I going to do?"

"Jayla?"

"I didn't even..."

"Jayla!" He yelled and snapped me out of it. I just fell into his arms.

Keon was so quiet, and I just finally got to his quiet. He calmed me down by being still and at ease. I took in a deep breath and walked to the kitchen. I looked for something to drink, but everything I had was just wine or Moscato. I needed something stronger than that.

"What am I going to do?" I started pacing the kitchen. I was getting antsy again. "What am I going to do Keon?"

"J, what are you talking about?" He looked at me. "I thought you were done with that married man," he said in a concerned tone.

I don't know how Keon even guessed that it about Darius, but I guess it wasn't such a shot in the dark. Keon was never a fan of Darius, and he hated that I was still seeing him. I know that I would say I was going to leave Darius, but I am in love with him. I thought I was going to live the rest of my life with him. Who knows what's going to happen now? What am I going to do?

"J, what is going on?" he asked me. "What has got you like this? What's got you all tied up?" I closed my eyes. I had to fight back the tears. I was trembling a little bit. I took in a deep breath and sighed. I opened my eyes and saw the look of concern on my brother's face. I had to get this out. I had to tell someone, and I think that Keon was the best person to say it to.

"I almost died, and it was at the hands of someone I longed to erase out of my life forever." I started to sob. "Keon, what have I gotten myself into?"

Chapter 1

Shenice

I took out my compact mirror and applied some lip gloss. I was waiting for Darius. We were going to have a late lunch together. It was rare that we did this. When we first started going out, we did it all the time. Even after we got married, we managed to move around our busy schedules and make sure that we ate with each other. So when he came out of nowhere and suggested for us to have lunch, I agreed.

"Hello gorgeous," he greeted me. He bent over and kissed me on the cheek. "You look and smell great today." He smiled. He sat down right across from me. He signaled for the waiter to come over. "I think that we're ready to order," he told the waiter. "Ladies first." He gave me his widest smile. I squinted at him but ordered anyway. He was so happy, and everything just seemed like the good old days. He ordered and then sent the waiter on his way. "I got so much to tell you."

Darius then went on to tell me about his day. His company landed three huge deals. First, he bought a beat-down building that he was going to renovate so that he could rent out the units. Secondly, he sold three multimillion-dollar homes. The final thing had him smiling so much that he could barely eat.

"What is it?" I asked, finishing up my salad. "You've been dragging out this thing, and I just want you to say what it is."

"Jamar's marketing...babe, he's such a marketing genius that he doesn't even see it. With some of the promotions he has done for the business, I've seen at least four times as many clients. There is so much business coming in, I don't know what to do. I might have to open up yet another location."

"That's a lot of new workers. Can you take on that many employees?"

"I know it's a bit much. That's why I was thinking of something else."

"There's even more?"

"I want to open up a real estate school," he told me, and my eyes opened wide. "Yeah, I want to open a real estate school."

"Wow."

"And to be honest, it's all because of you."

"Me?"

"You were the person who introduced me to this real estate life. Without you, who knows where I would be. I just want to do for someone what you did for me."

It was times like these that I fell in love with Darius all over again. If he wasn't a serial cheater and a liar, we could have had forever. We could have had all the vows. I tried to live by the vows at first. When he first cheated, I thought I could just ignore it, but this thing with this new bitch, I can't do it no more. I'm at my wits' end. And as much as I loved Darius, I refused to be a fool over him anymore.

"I'm just trying for us to move forward. I would love if you would be a part of this school."

"Really?" I was shocked. "What would I be doing?"

"You could teach, or you could even just help with bringing in students. I know sometimes you feel like I just turned you into this housewife, and in a lot of ways, I did. So maybe in some way I can get you out there and work."

"Are you serious?" My eyes started to get a little misty.

"Yeah. I think you'd be a great asset."

A tear slid down my cheek. I used to tell Darius this all the time. I used to tell him that I loved being a wife and mother, but I wanted to do more. Now that our five-year-old daughter was in school, I felt incomplete. I had nothing to do in the mornings. I spent a lot of my time shopping, which was cool, but there was only so much shopping I could do. I wanted to do something constructive. To hear him actually have something for me to do, I felt a bit overwhelmed. If only it could always be like this. If only he didn't have to cheat. Then I wouldn't be in this position.

My phone started to vibrate. I looked down, and the phone number caught my attention.

"I got to take this phone call. You know my mom." I rolled my eyes. I got up and went towards the exit.

"Hey," I whispered into the phone. "Is everything set up?"

"Of course. I'm just calling to make sure that you don't back down from it. The last thing I need is for you to feel that you want me to end. Like I always tell you, once I get this started, I cannot stop it. So I don't need you saying to stop it."

"I understand."

"So yes? Do you want me to do this favor for you?"

I looked back into the restaurant and saw Darius. He was sitting there with his phone out. He was probably texting that bitch. One minute he was talking about me and him and this whole school thing. One minute he was telling me that he wanted to renew everything between us and that he wanted us to work out. One minute he was already promising to be a better man, and now look at him. Now he was smiling and looking down at his phone. He was texting that bitch one second and promising me the world in the other. Fucking piece of shit.

"I'm sure. You do what I told you to do, and don't mess up."

"I never mess up, and you know that."

"Yes, I do know that." I smiled.

"I'll speak with you after."

"Ok Goodbye."

"Bye."

I ended the phone call and went back to Darius. I smiled and acted like everything was okay.

"How is your mom?" he asked, with his face looking concerned. "Is everything okay?"

"You know my mother. She can be so dramatic sometimes. She can take the smallest problem in the world and make it seem like it's the end of the world."

"I know. Some of the stories you tell me..." He shook his head and started chuckling. "Some of them are just so crazy."

"That's Mother for you." I sighed. "So, are you ready to go?" I asked. "I want to go check up on my mom."

"I thought you said it was nothing."

"It isn't, but you know her Darius. She is just going to find something else for her to be dramatic about. I don't want me to keep interrupting our lunch date just to be picking up the phone."

"You know what? You are absolutely right. But now that I think about it, I got to get back to the office."

"I'm sure." I gave him a sly smile.

He signaled the waiter again. He told him that he wanted the check. Then he did something so strange. He reached out and held my hand. It struck me so hard.

"I'm really trying to change," he told me. Had I not heard this a million times before, I might have believed him. If this was my first time hearing this, maybe he and I could have made it work, but that was not the case. I'd seen him do it all and I'd heard it all. I'm done with the bullshit.

"I'll see you when you get home."

He paid for the late lunch and then helped me out of my chair. He kissed me on the cheek and then softly on my lips. I closed my eyes and smiled. I was holding back my hate. I had to pretend that everything was okay. When we got outside, the valet handed me my car keys and opened the door for me.

"Love you." Darius was surprising me with all this affection.

"I love you too." I kissed his cheek and got in the car. I pulled off but went someplace close. I could still see Darius. He was now on his phone. He didn't even wait five or ten minutes before he started talking to that ho. How could I feel sorry for this dude when he treated me like this? He was playing with my heart like it was nothing. He was falling for this bitch and not giving a fuck about our family. Why should I give a fuck then? Why should I fucking care? Why is it my burden? I'm going to fix him.

I saw a car and looked closely and saw him. It was Trey. He looked over and saw me and nodded. It was time. It was time for it all to go down. Darius got in his car and drove off. He didn't see us at all. He was on his way to that slut probably. I could bet my life on it.

I followed behind Darius, and I could see in my rearview that Trey was behind me. We kept going and going. He finally got to this place, and there the bitch was. That slut ran up in front of him and he grabbed her in for a passionate kiss. He squeezed her ass, and you could see his wide smile from here. I shook my head and felt myself trembling in anger. He opened the car door for her, and they went off. We followed them some more, and then we saw his car pull up by this bar. They got out and were walking hand-in-hand into the bar.

There was a knock on my car window. I jumped up but sighed in relief when I saw Trey.

"What are you doing?" he asked.

"You know what the crazy thing is?" I completely ignored his question. "I'm so used to following Darius that I don't even notice I'm doing it anymore." I was staring blankly out the window. "It's almost normal for me to get out and follow Darius," I confessed. "Isn't that the saddest thing that you ever heard?" A tear rolled down my cheek. "Isn't it so fucking sad? Isn't it sad that this is what the fuck I have to do?"

It got really quiet. The tears that I shed came out of anger. I hated what Darius had done to me. He had turned me into something that I didn't even recognize.

"I'm going to ask you again, and please really try to think about it. Are you sure that you want to do this?" he asked me, and looked me in the eyes. I wiped my angry tears away.

"I am. I'm so ready for all of this to be over." I sighed.

"I got you."

Jayla

The smooth jazz songs on the jukebox were so sexy, or maybe it was just my man. We were at this great bar, and it was so seductive. I really missed Darius, and when he sent me a text message saying that he wanted to see me, of course I got ready. I had to ignore Keon calling me a dummy for the umpteenth time. I was in love with Darius and he was in love with me. One of these days, when all the dust settled, Keon would see that Darius was a standup guy. He would see us become a family, and then I could see everything else fall into place.

"You are so sexy." Darius leaned in and nibbled my ear. I had a few drinks, but it was obvious that Darius had one too many.

"Are you okay baby?" I asked him, because he was all over me.

"I'm good." He smiled. "I just missed you so much."

"You did?" I blushed.

"I really did babe." He grabbed me close and kissed me. "You don't get how much I miss you. I hate when I don't get to see you all the time."

"But hopefully that will change, right?" I looked at him, expecting an answer. I knew he was a bit drunk, and usually drunk people told the truth. I was going to take advantage of the situation and see what he said.

"It is going to be soon. Everything will be fine. I'm trying my best."

I didn't quite get his answer, but I just took in the fact that he was trying. I knew that Darius and I would be together officially, and it was nice to hear that he was trying.

"I love you." He grabbed me and kissed me again.

"We got to get out of here." I giggled.

"Yeah. Let's go back to your place. Or maybe we go to a hotel." He gave me that knowing smile. I giggled some more and shook my head. "We can just get in the car and go. I mean we can just go."

"No Darius. You are in no condition to drive. I think we should take a nice walk."

"Yes, a nice, romantic walk. We used to go on romantic walks." He winked. "Remember after we got your steak?"

"Yes."

"I want to do that again." He took my hand and laced his fingers with mine. I nodded my head, and he slapped some money down to pay for everything. I figured that the night air could only help sober him up.

There was a park nearby, and we decided that the park was the best place for this romantic walk. He was holding my hand, and I felt like we were young lovers. For some reason, everything felt brand new. It was like we were dating all over again. Darius looked at me like he did the first time he saw me. He kissed the back of my hand as we started making our way to the park. I looked up at the night sky and thought that this night couldn't get more perfect.

Suddenly behind us, we heard footsteps. We turned around and saw someone with a hood over their face running towards us. Darius gripped my hand and held it tightly. By the look on Darius's face, he was 100 percent sober now. His face was hard, and whatever was coming at us, he was going to protect me.

The person ran up to us and pulled out a gun. I took two steps back, and out of nowhere, there was a strong wind. The strong breeze lifted the hood off the mysterious person's face. He turned away for a half second, but when he turned back, I got a good look at his face.

"Oh shit," I cursed. I started to tremble. "It's you." I pointed at him. "It's you?" I looked him up and down. "What are you doing?"

"You know him?" Darius asked, and before I could nod, he pointed the gun at us and shot.

"Darius!!" I screamed as the gunman ran away after he shot us.

"I'm okay. He missed. Let's get the fuck out of here."

He grabbed my hand and we headed for the car. I looked behind us and saw the gunman coming after us.

"Oh fuck," I whispered, but luckily we were right by the car.

"Get in! Get fucking in!" Darius shouted, and we got in.

"Drive off."

Darius turned on the engine and pulled off before the guy could even get to us.

Chapter 2

Trey

I watched the car pull off and leave.

"Fuck!" I shouted. How could I have fucked up so bad? It's like as soon as that breeze hit me, it threw my whole game up. I've never screwed up a hit. I was usually up close, pulling a trigger, but then gone like nothing had happened. This is so fucked up, and on top of that, that bitch recognized me. I got to finish this. Because if I didn't, I might end up getting locked up.

"What the fuck!" Shenice came running out to me. "You didn't even get off a shot. You didn't hit. You fucking missed!"

"I know. You don't have to give me the play-by-play. I was there. I saw what happened. I fucked up. The wind—"

"The wind! The fucking wind! You mean to tell me you messed up this whole thing because of the wind?" she screamed, shaking her head at me. "You fucking idiot. Do you know—"

"Yeah, I fucking know." I grabbed her. "Like I said, you are not telling me something that I don't already fucking know," I told her gruffly. "Now how about you lower your fucking voice before someone hears you?"

"I'm sorry," she pleaded. I let her go.

"You got me fucked up."

I started to make my way to the car. Shenice was right behind me. I'd calmed her down when I'd grabbed her, but she was still nervous.

"She is going to put this all together. That fucking bitch." She was still shaking her head. "She saw me with Jamar, so she is going to put it all together. She is going to know that this is because of that. She is going to link this all back to me. I know she is." She was shaking. "I know she is."

"I'll take care of it." I opened my car's driver door.

"What do you mean?"

"I'm going to finish the job. That's what you paid me to do, and I'm going to do it."

That was when I saw all the color leave her face. She was so shocked at what I had said, but I meant it. I can't let this go, especially not after the fact she recognized who I was. She looked at me and pointed me out. For all I know, she was in that car telling that nigga everything about me. I can't let this go on. I have to find them and end it right now.

"No. Don't do that." It was almost like Shenice could read my thoughts.

"What? Don't forget, you're the one that put me out on this. How are you going to hire me and then take it all back?"

"That was only after the mistake had been made. We can't do this no more. We have to let it go."

"You are afraid of the bitch finding out it was you. Look, if we do this, at least we can have that off our heads. I need to end this now."

"No." She shook her head. "It's gone too far now."

"Too far? Bitch, we're talking about fucking murder," I whispered. "What the fuck did you think you were hiring me for? What do you think is going to happen now? You think that this will all blow over? You think they are just going to let that go?"

"No, they won't." She started to nod. She was coming to her senses. "That bitch knows a lot about me. If I let this go, she's just going to tie it to me anyway. She's just going to go after me."

"So I got to finish this."

"You're right." Shenice started walking to her car. "Do what you have to do!"

Darius

I can't believe what just happened. After dropping Jayla home, I just took a small drive around. Was I just almost killed? That man just brought a gun up to me and Jayla and pulled the trigger. If it wasn't for the wind, we would have been dead. When the wind distracted him, it basically saved our lives. What the fuck? I tried to speak with Jayla, but she was just so frantic. She wasn't much help. I knew once she calmed down we'd really get to talk, but for now I would just leave it alone.

I got home and crashed on my couch. I tried to calm down, but my mind was still racing. Everything was happening so fast. My heart was still racing, and I was starting to sweat. I went to the fridge to get something to drink.

"Darius?" Shenice's voice made me jump. I turned and saw her wearing a robe. "What's going on? You seem so nervous."

A part of me wanted to tell her what was going on. I mean, even though I messed around, Shenice was my wife. She always had a good head on her shoulders. She would often give me good advice and tell me where to go. But since I was with Jayla, there was no way that I could bring this up.

"Just work," I lied with a half smile. "This client..." I couldn't even think of a lie quick enough. Usually I could come up with something quickly, but now I was too shaken up. I just looked away into the fridge and hoped that she would go away.

"A client?" She walked farther into the kitchen. "Tell me all about it. You know that I would love to help."

"No babe. It's okay." I sighed. I noticed that it was really quiet. "The baby is asleep?"

"No. She's at my mother's place."

"You went out?"

For some strange reason, she froze. She just looked at me so weirdly. It was as if she wasn't expecting me to ask that question.

"What's wrong with you? I just asked a simple question and you turned to stone."

"It's not that Darius. I'm just tired. I didn't go out; I just wanted some time to myself."

"Are you okay?" I asked.

"Yeah, I'm cool. I guess I might be coming down with something. Don't worry about it."

"Of course I'm going to worry about it; you're my wife." I smiled.

Out of nowhere, she hugged me tightly. I thought it was weird, but considering the type of day I had, I needed a hug. It felt nice.

"I'm going to head to bed. You coming?" She was already on the way there.

"Sure. I'm just going to get something to drink real quick. I just need to calm my nerves."

"That client really got you shook," she called out from the other room.

"You have no idea," I whispered.

When I heard the bedroom door close, I got my phone and called Jayla. Maybe she would have calmed down by now.

"Hello?" She still sound scared and nervous, but that was perfectly normal.

"I just wanted to check up on you to see if you're okay."

"I am not okay."

"I know."

"That was fucking crazy. We almost died Darius."

"I know. I still can't wrap my head around it. How the fuck—" I cut myself off. "Out of all the random shit that has happened in my life..."

"But here's the thing: I don't think it's random."

I almost dropped the phone right there and then. What did she mean by that? "What? What are you talking about Jayla? What happened to us was random."

"No. I don't think so at all."

"Explain."

"I will tell you when I see you."

I wanted to push it further, but the more I thought about it, I realized that it was best. I couldn't talk about this with Shenice at home. What if she overheard me and wondered who Jayla was? It was smart to just wait on this.

"We'll find a time to talk about all of this." I took a deep breath. "I was just calling to check up on you. I know we just went through something crazy, but don't get so carried away with it. Keep the doors locked and all that." I was just pulling things out of my ass to comfort her. I was still messed up, but I knew that I had to be strong for her.

"Okay," she said in a small voice.

"I love you," I told her.

"I love you too." Her voice picked up a bit more spirit, but I knew she was still down.

I ended the phone call and shook my head. What a night.

Trey

I wasn't a person that liked to drink hard liquor, but when I got back to my house, I was guzzling back a bottle of Hennessey. I couldn't believe I had fucked this up. I had to make this right. I had to complete it, and it was not even about Shenice anymore. I had to do it because she saw my face and could identify me to whoever, and I couldn't afford that. I had a rep for being efficient, and I was not going to let this mistake fuck it all up.

My phone started blowing up. I looked down and saw Shenice's name light up my screen. It was four in the morning. What was she doing calling me so late?

"What's up?" I asked, wiping the liquor off my face.

"Hey Trey." Her voice was kind of shaky and she was kind of whispering.

"Where are you?" It was really quiet in the background, but I could kind of hear cars every now and then.

"I am in my car, and I was wondering if I could meet up with you."

"Right now?"

"Yes, please."

I wasn't in the mood, but I had a feeling that she wasn't going to stop calling me until I agreed. She was just going to keep going. As much as I didn't want to see her, I didn't need that type of aggravation.

"Whatever." I shrugged my shoulders. "I'll send you directions to the place where we can see each other."

After getting a quick shower, I hopped in the car. My driver was already there. He was so reliable like that. It didn't matter what time I called him over; he was always ready for whatever. He never complained and just did what he was told. That's why I kept him around.

"You got the address that I texted you?" I asked as I strapped on my seat belt.

"Yeah."

"Let's go."

We drove until we got to this twenty-four hour diner. It was practically empty if you didn't include the staff. I saw Shenice there wearing shades and a scarf. She was being so fucking dramatic. What did she think this was?

"What's going on?" I sat in the booth. "What do you need to talk about?" She was looking around like she was waiting for someone to pop up. She was so scared. "I don't got all fucking day for this, so get to it."

"I think we should just drop this whole thing."

"No," I told her immediately. "That is not even an option."

"Why not?" Her eyes were open wide. "This whole thing is a big mess. Don't you think that it would be best for you to back down from this whole thing?"

"We already spoke about this." I leaned back. "I didn't come here for us to fucking rehash old news. I'm going to do this, and that's the end of that."

"No. I think that if you go through with this, we are all going to get caught." She leaned forward and whispered it.

"Please. I don't make mistakes," I replied in a cocky manner.

"But you already did."

I got real quiet. She was right about that. It was hard to argue with someone when they were right. I fucked up tonight, but it won't happen again.

"I get it." I blew out air. I had to say what she wanted to hear. She was starting to bother me, and I figured if I played her game, she would leave me alone. "Maybe I should back off."

"Yes." Her eyes twinkled.

"And just let this whole thing go." I kept acting like I was done with it, but that wasn't true at all. I will finish what I started.

"Yes. You let it go." She let out a huge breath of relief. "But I will do it."

"What?"

"You have to back off and be safe, but I think I should handle this from now on."

"You?"

"Yes, me."

I wanted to laugh out loud, but I had to play my cards close to my chest. If I was going to act like I wasn't interested in it anymore, I had to go along with it. But if Shenice thinks that she can do what I do, she is an idiot. Everybody can kill, but it's not like everybody can do it well. Some people just can't do it. I don't think Shenice knows what she is up for. She may think that she is street smart, but just by looking at her, I know that she isn't. If she was really about that life, she would have taken care of it herself in the first place.

"If you think that is best." I stood up, pretending like I was on board with her decision. "I got to go. I got money to make," I added.

"I understand." She stood up. She seemed even more relieved now. She wasn't as paranoid like she was before. I threw down fifty dollars on the table. Although we didn't have anything to eat or drink, I knew us holding up the table could have stopped them from making money. I just liked everyone to make money. The waitress didn't hesitate to come and snatch it up either.

"Thank you." The waitress smiled and went on her way.

"I'm so glad that you understand," Shenice told me while we were outside. I just nodded my head and got back into the car.

"Where to?" my driver asked as he started the engine.

"Back to the crib." He pulled away, and I saw Shenice drive away.

"So did everything go okay?" His eyes looked at me using the rearview mirror.

"Yeah it did. I had to play stupid and pretend that I wasn't going to kill a person." I yawned.

"Oh, you are not doing that job anymore?"

"Fuck outta here. Of course I'm still killing them. You know me; I can't keep no loose ends."

"You just told her that you wasn't going to do it."

"And that's all the information she needed to know," I told my driver. "When I say I'm going to take care of something, I mean it."

Chapter 3

Darius

It was really a long day at work. As much as I tried to put my head into the game, I couldn't. I just kept flashing back to when I had the gun in my face, the gunshot going off, and the sound of my tires peeling off in the wind. It was something that would never leave my memory. Every time I even tried to move on from it, I was back to that moment: Jayla freaking out, me grabbing her hand, and the look of death in the gunman's eyes. What the fuck?

I was just staring at the computer screen. I knew I was supposed to do something, but each time I started, I just forgot. I had my mind still on that gun. What if that person hadn't missed? What if they hit me? I could be dead right now. My daughter would grow up without a father. That thought terrified me. I put my head down on the desk and tried to collect my thoughts.

"Are you okay?" Jamar's voice was puzzled. He sounded as if he was genuinely concerned. He was sitting at his desk, opposite of mine. "You've been quiet all day. You haven't even been out to go to meetings or to make money, which is not like you. And now you're just resting your head on the table. What is going on?" I began to open my mouth, but the words wouldn't come out. "What is it?"

"I can't even get into it." I sighed. "Just a whole bunch of bullshit, and I don't want you to worry about it."

"How are you going to say that? You know what, you better tell me. Let me know. You know that you and I are like brothers, and as your brother, you should tell me what's going on with you. The way you are acting right now, it's got me worried."

"I know, but it's just so much that I don't even know where to start."

"What about you start at the beginning? Don't rush through it. Just tell me every detail, because you've been keeping it in, and it's not working for you."

"I guess you're right."

"So, tell me what's going on with you. Just let me know."

I sighed and thought about it some more. I leaned back in my office chair. This was really weighing on me. Jamar could tell, and even Shenice could. When I woke up this morning to get ready for breakfast, she was trying to get me to open up, but I couldn't tell her. What was I supposed to say?

"Hey honey, while I was out there cheating on you, I almost was killed. Can you come here and comfort me while not being mad at the fact that I was cheating?" Yeah, that's not likely. But Jamar knows about my dirt, so I should tell him.

"Well, it starts like this—" My phone vibrating interrupted me. I was going to ignore it like I did my other clients' calls, but when I saw it was Jayla, I picked it up. "Hey babe. How you doing?"

"Just...it's so much." She sounded just like me. It was clear that she had the same weight on her shoulders like I did. "How long before I can see you?"

"What?" I looked at my watch. It was only 3 p.m. "Did you go to work today? It's so early, so I know that you can't be getting off work."

"No. I took the day off," she explained. "I didn't think that I should work when I feel like this."

"That's a good idea; honestly I should have done the same."

"You're at work?"

"Yeah. I'm here in the office with Jamar right now."

"Can I see you?" She sounded urgent.

It was weird to hear her sound so panicked, but I guess with all that has went down, it should make sense.

"When I get off work, would that be good?"

"No. Right now Darius." She said it in a firm tone. She never really spoke to me like that, so I knew that it had to be urgent.

"Okay. I'll see you right now."

"I'll send you the info in a few." She then ended the call.

"What was that about?" Jamar asked. I started to stand up.

"I'm leaving."

"You leaving? You barely did any work today."

"I know, but I got to get out of here. I'm not in the right frame of mind to do this shit," I confessed. "My ass should have stayed at home."

"Are you really leaving?"

"Yeah."

"But what about the story you were going to tell me? You just going to leave and not tell me a thing?"

"I got to go."

"But at least come back and tell me."

"I'll try."

I was out of the office, and in a few seconds I received a text message from Jayla. She wanted us to meet at a local coffee place that wasn't so far from her home. I got in the car and drove off. I blasted some music and tried to zone out. I was still a bit antsy, but I had to get in the right frame of mind. I didn't want Jayla to see that I was a bit panicked and start to feel more uneasy. I had to stand strong for her.

When I got to the coffee place, seeing Jayla in her sweats with hair pulled back, I was amazed at how beautiful she was. She was so gorgeous, but in those eyes, you could still see the fear.

"Hey." I sat down and she jumped a little. "Are you okay?"

"To be honest, I'm real fucked up." She rubbed the temples of her head.

"Did you get anything to eat?" She shook her head, and I got up to order us some food. When I got back, I had her cup of green tea, a croissant, a yogurt, and two bacon and eggs sandwiches. "Here you go." I set the tray down, but she didn't make any moves. "You need to eat."

"I don't think I can." She breathed out deeply. She played with the food, but when she looked at me and saw how serious I was, she took a nibble of the food. "There. Are you happy?"

"I'll take what I can get." I handed her the yogurt and a spoon. "Now eat."

We had a small lunch. We didn't talk much. When we were finished, I cleared the table.

"I know it's been crazy, but how have you been?" I asked her. She just shrugged her shoulders. "Tell me." I reached out and held her hand. The troubled look in her eyes stuck something in me. "What is it Jayla?" I gave her hand a slight squeeze to let her know that I was still here for her.

"I don't think what happened to us the other night was random at all." She said these words slowly, and I could see this boulder of guilt lift off her shoulders. She let out this huge sigh of relief, but there was a part of her that was still worried.

"What do you mean? I remember you saying this the other night, but I don't know what you are talking about." I said to her, but she didn't say anything else. "What are you trying to say Jayla? Are you trying to say that we were set up?" She nodded her head. "That's ridiculous. Who would set us up?"

"Your wife."

"Shenice?" I shook my head, because I didn't agree with her. "No. Shenice wouldn't do that."

"Yes she would, and she wasn't alone in setting you up."

"What do you mean?"

"It was her and Jamar."

I pushed away from the table. I got up and started walking away.

"I'm not into these games Jayla," I told her over my shoulder. "I thought you were going to tell me something useful, but you here telling me some fucking bullshit." I spun around. "Is this what you're resorting to? Are you sick and tired of waiting, so you have to make up stories? I'm going to leave my wife, so why did you feel the need to make up this story?"

"I'm not." She reached out to me, and I began to pull away. "Look at me Darius," she said in that same firm tone she had used before. I looked in her eyes and saw the truth. I saw that she wasn't lying at all. "Come on. Let's go for a walk."

We walked around the block. She was quiet at first, but maybe that was a good thing. My mind was racing with what she had just told me.

"You remember that time we went to dinner and you asked me what was wrong with me?" I gave her a confused look to her question. "You kept trying to get me to open up, and I just kept telling you that I was okay and was alright. Do you remember that night?"

I thought back to that dinner where she barely said a word. Yeah, I remembered that night. Something in me had told me she was holding back about something, but I honestly thought it was something to do with her brother Keon, or maybe even her job. When she told me that everything was good, I let it go only a little bit. I thought that if it was anything bad, she would eventually tell me. Maybe this is what she is doing.

"Yes, I remember. So..."

"So, once I went grocery shopping, and I saw someone who looked familiar. Once I got closer to the person, I saw that it was your wife, Shenice. I knew it was her, because when she came up to your condo that night, I snuck a peek at her. Plus, I've seen a photo of her at your office."

"You saw my wife. Why didn't you tell me?"

"Because I saw her with Jamar."

"They are friends. Besides, they might have just bumped into each other and just hung out."

"I would have thought that too if it wasn't for the way they were acting together."

"And how was that?"

"They were a couple. They were so lovey-dovey that it shocked me. It was like..." She stopped talking.

She was silent and kept walking. She had her eyes closed. I was about to press her for more, but I didn't. I knew she was going to give me more details, but she was just taking her time. I had to be patient, but it was killing me. My wife and my best friend be involved together like that; they just can't.

"I know what a couple looks like, and they were a couple. On top of all of that, they were coming out of a lingerie store."

"What?" I screwed up a face. "She hasn't bought any lingerie," I told her. "Every time Shenice buys new lingerie, she models it for me or she takes a picture of herself in it for me. I haven't gotten any new pictures."

"Maybe the lingerie she bought wasn't for you." She worded herself cautiously. "Maybe it was for Jamar."

"You're crazy." I dismissed her. "Just because you saw them together outside some store, now you think that they are—" I cut myself off. "Man, not even."

"But that wasn't it. There is actually more."

I took a short stop. I didn't know how much information I could take, but I knew that if she told me this much, she might as well tell me it all.

"What else?"

"Well I saw them again that night, but this time at a gas station. She was all over him while they were getting gas." I was stunned. "And then they kissed each other...on the lips."

"Really?"

"And then they saw me."

"They saw you."

"Well, I was driving really slowly so I could get a good look at them. I had to make sure it was them for real. And somehow they spotted me. They started to walk towards my car and I just drove off.

And when I looked in the rearview, I could see them arguing."

"That's crazy."

"I think it was them that set this whole thing up. I think this is all to make sure that I didn't tell you anything."

I was about to dispute her, but then I thought back to Shenice and Jamar, but especially Jamar. There was that night he took me out for drinks and just kept asking all these questions about Jayla and Shenice. He kept warning me and telling me that one day I was going pay for all that I have done. Was this what he was talking about? Was he trying to tell me something, or was he just laughing at all that I had done?

"I think you're right," I said out of nowhere. "One time Jamar just kept questioning me, but I thought nothing of it. But now thinking about it..." I got quiet. "But he's supposed to be my brother." After I said those words, Jayla took me into her arms. She hugged me tight and close while rubbing my back. That's what made it feel like she was really telling me the truth. She was comforting me, and I was taking it all in.

Jamar and Shenice? They'd always had this playful relationship, but I would have never thought that they would be together. It was always along the lines of family, but never anything sexual. Maybe that was how it all started. Maybe it was just friendly at first and then they got carried away. I wondered how long they'd been together. When did it all start? When? And when did they decide that I had to be permanently taken out of the picture? When did they come together and contemplate my murder?

"Darius?" Jayla looked at me. "Are you okay? I know I just gave you a lot of information, but seeing as how everything went down the other night, I don't think I should hold this in anymore."

"I don't blame you." I took a deep breath. "I don't blame you," I repeated. "I just can't believe it, but I know it's true."

"I'm sorry."

"It's not your fault. I just have to get to the bottom of this."

"What do you mean?"

"I'm going to find out."

"You're going to confront him?" she asked, and I nodded my head. "You're not worried?"

I thought about it and then shook my head.

"Why not?"

"Because the sad thing is that as much as I am mad, the truth of the matter is, I'm so disappointed. I can get why Shenice could get so mad, but damn, Jamar is like my brother. He was just telling me today that we are like brothers, and to think that my so-called brother could do that to me is kind of disturbing. He was seriously acting like he was there for me..." I stood up straight. "I got to go."

"You're going to do this now?"

"There's no time better than the present." I walked to my car and hit the button to disable the alarm. I opened the car door and sat inside.

"Wait." Jayla held the door open and tried to stop me. "Take some time to cool off. You can't go there like this."

"Why not?"

"Just think about it."

"I've thought about it enough." I reached out and closed the door. I brought the window down and looked at her. "I love you." I then started the engine and drove off.

Chapter 4

Darius

I hated to leave Jayla like that, but the information she gave me didn't sit well with me. I raced through these Atlanta streets, not giving a fuck about the speed limit. I just wanted to get to Jamar and confront him. I'm going to try real hard to not put my hands on him, but I'm not going to make any promises.

Walking into the office, I must have looked like the devil, because a lot of the real estate sales associates that worked for me stayed clear of me. Usually they would wave or smile, but they were just moving out of the way. I walked to my office and saw Jamar talking to one of the female employees. They were going over some files or something.

"Hey, what's up?" Jamar asked as I breezed past him.

"In my office...now," I told him, and I went to wait for him to follow me. Once he got into the office, I closed and locked the door behind him.

"What is going on?"

"How long have you been fucking my wife Jamar?"

His eyes opened wide, and then he stopped and had a little smile on his face.

"What are you talking about man? Have you been drinking?" He gave an awkward laugh.

"I just asked you a simple question Jamar." I started walking towards him. "How long have you been fucking my wife?"

"Are you crazy?" He laughed some more. "You over here looking all types of insane right now, and then you come to me with this crazy question."

"Answer the fucking question. Are you fucking my wife?" I was inches away from his face. "I swear Jamar, if you keep ducking and dodging my fucking question, I will lay you out on this floor right now."

"Really?"

"Yes fucking really. So I am going to ask you this question one more fucking time: Are you fucking my wife?"

Jamar just looked at me like I was going nuts, but I was.

"You know the answer to that. I'm not fucking your wife." He looked me right in the eye and lied. Jayla already gave me the truth, and I knew that she had no reason to lie. She had no reason to tell me such an outlandish story. When she told me the story, she looked me right in the eyes, and I just knew that she was telling me the truth. Right now, with Jamar inches away from my face, I knew for a fact that he was lying.

"How long have we known each other? Almost our whole fucking lives right?" I questioned Jamar. "How could you do this to me?"

"What are you talking about? I just answered your question. I told you that I'm not sleeping with Shenice." I rolled my eyes upward. "So what you are trying to say is that you don't believe me?"

"No, I don't fucking believe you. I'm looking at you right now, and I can tell that you're lying."

"You're being paranoid."

"Me? Paranoid? I've known you for all our lives. Don't you think I know when you're lying?"

"You're tripping."

He tried to make it for the door, but I blocked his way.

"You really want to talk about this bullshit? You really want to be here and argue about something that ain't' true? You really think that I would do that to you."

"I know that you have!" I shouted. "You've been fucking my wife, and then you have a fucking nerve to act like you're concerned for me."

"Oh God...this is such bullshit."

"I've known you for all this time, and you are acting like I can't tell when you're lying. I know when you're lying, and you're lying to me right now."

"I am not!" He raised his voice.

"Yes, you are motherfucker! I just want to know how long."

"How long?"

"Yes! How long? How long have you and my wife had this thing going on? Was this before or after Jayla?"

"Jayla? What the fuck..." He started walking backward. "Let me guess, this has something to do with her?"

"No, it doesn't."

"I can bet money that she was the one who planted this idea in your head."

"Shut up." I brushed him off.

Jamar just chuckled.

"You are fucking something else Darius. Now with all your dogging around on your wife—"

"Dogging around?"

"I'm just calling a spade a motherfucking spade. You've been doing wrong by Shenice, and now you are feeling guilty about it. So instead of being a man and doing right by her, you have to be a bitch and throw all this dirt on me."

"If I were you, I'd watch your mouth, nigga."

His eyes opened extremely wide. I rarely cursed, and I rarely used slang. It was just not something I do all the time, but when I'm angry, anything goes. Knowing that Jamar was having sex with my wife was bad, but knowing that he was lying to my face was really pissing me off. I couldn't even get into the whole murder thing, because it looked like he wasn't trying to say anything. It seemed he was going to keep this lie up until forever.

"I never thought that you could do this to me. How could you even accuse me of this shit, all out of what your sidechick told you? You think she not trying to get you to leave your wife? I told you that she was going to get tired of that shit. Now look. She's trying to tear you apart and you are letting it happen."

"The only thing she did was tell me the truth about my so-called brother. You still going to stand there and lie to me?"

"I'm not lying."

"Well I don't believe you."

"Sad to say, but there is nothing I can do to change that. If you can't take what I've been telling, then it's really going to be a waste of breath. We've known each other for practically our whole lives, but you're really going to take what some chick that you've known for a second says over me? There's nothing else for me to say."

Jamar unlocked the office and walked out. I sat down in my office chair and huffed. I saw his desk right across from mine and got angry all over again. I got up and called out to one of my secretaries.

"You know that empty office we have down the hall?" I asked her.

"Yes, sure. You were saying the other day that you were going to find something to do with it," she reminded me.

"I have." I turned to Jamar's things. "Please have someone come and move all of these things into that office. That will be his new office from now on."

"Really? I'm so used to seeing you two work so closely together."

"I didn't ask for your opinion. I just told you to move his things." I went back to my desk.."Can you get to that ASAP please?"

She called for the custodial and maintenance staff members to come upstairs. They began packing up Jamar's things and I just got to work. I had been getting distracted all day, and I couldn't let that happen any longer. My personal life may have been falling apart, but I was not going to let my business suffer. I set up some appointments with potential clients. I emailed other clients digital photos and videos of various properties throughout Atlanta. The more I got into my work, the better I would feel. Sometimes work was the best distraction there was.

"You really moving my shit clear across the other side of the building?" Jamar stormed into my office. He bumped into some of the workers. They didn't stop packing his stuff up. Even though Jamar was the head of marketing, everyone in this company knew that I was the boss. When it came down to me and him, I was the one they had to listen to. I stood up and got in his face again.

"Of course I fucking did. Did you really think that I was going to have you in my face while you are fucking my wife?" I looked at him like he was crazy. "You must have lost your mind."

"It's come to this."

"Yes, it's come to this."

"But you are supposed to be my brother."

"You ain't no brother of mine." I glared at him up and down.

"Now we not even brothers?"

"Nope." I shook my head. "We not brothers; we not even fucking friends. You and I are just business associates." I let him know how I felt.

We were nose to nose. It almost felt like we were going to fight, but then he backed away, shaking his head. He picked up a few of his things and left. The rest of the day there was this huge tension between us. The rest of the workers picked up on it. I was sure they were all gossiping about what was going on. Who knows? Maybe they had even heard us, because during some of our dispute, we were yelling a lot of it. When I walked out of my office, people got quiet and went back to work. I walked past Jamar's new office. He was still in the middle of setting it up when he saw me looking at him. He tried to smile, but I just walked forward and closed his door. I don't have time for this bullshit. I had a business to take care of and run.

Chapter 5

Jayla

After Darius left me in the middle of the street, I was so conflicted. Where on one side I was happy that I finally told him about his friend and his wife, but on the other side, I was so messed up. Maybe I should have kept it to myself, but it had been eating at me for a long time. Ever since I saw Jamar with Shenice, I've been holding this huge secret to myself. When I would see Darius, it took everything in me to not tell him. It was after we almost died together when I realized I should tell him. It was just too much of a coincidence that one day I went from seeing Shenice and Jamar together and then a few days down the line I was almost dying.

Shenice and Jamar must have been plotting this for a while. I remember when Jamar reached out to Kim. He invited us out, but I turned it down. I guess after he saw that he couldn't get to me that way, him and Shenice cooked up a new plan to get to me. I think they thought long and hard about it and just thought that killing me was the best solution to keep their secret. So much drama.

I tried to keep myself busy with work, like always. Charmaine and Kim kept me laughing and in stitches, but it wasn't enough for me to forget about all my troubles. Yesterday at work, Charmaine and Kim were so happy when I got there. I didn't even clock in yet and they were damn near jumping up and down.

Flashback:

"What is going on?" I asked them after I finally clocked in. "You guys are so happy for people that are just clocking in for work. Charmaine and Kim exchanged looks. "Damn, what is it? If it's good news, I could use some good news."

"What type of drama do you have going on in your life?" Kim asked, and I just shook my head. I wasn't going to tell them. I knew if I did that they would just worry their heads off. There was no point in making them go crazy.

"Nothing, just regular shit." I gave them a smile. "You know me and Keon bump heads every now and then," I lied. "But enough about that. What has got you here grinning like a little kid at Disney World?"

"Girrrrrrllllllll," Charmaine said in a way only she knew how, "I got the best thing for you today. What would make you really happy right now at work? Like, what would be the best thing for the work space right now?"

"Did we all get a raise?" I asked, and then their smiles started to fade.

"Shit, that would have been nice," Kim commented and then laughed. "Okay, so maybe not the best thing that could happen." They both laughed out loud. "What would be something nice?"

"I don't know."

"Nicki is not here," they both said at the same time.

A smile grew across my face. Nicki was our supervisor, and at times it felt like she thought she was President Obama or something. She would make us do things that were so extra and have an attitude to match. It was hard working under her, but because I had fun with Charmaine and Kim all the time, it was bearable.

"She's not here?" I walked around the building just to make sure. I greeted our other coworkers and staff. When I saw that they were smiling too, I knew it wasn't bullshit. "She really is not here?" I smiled wider. "Damn, it's nice to have one thing go my way."

"Okay, that is the second time you said some shit like that. What is going on? And don't even try to give us that stupid nothing is going on nonsense."

"No really, nothing is going on." I tried to reassure them. "I am just tired."

"You're tired?" Charmaine's tone was letting me know that she didn't believe me.

"Yeah seriously." I gave another fake smile.

"I thought you said that it was things with your brother." Kim squinted her eyes at me. "So, which one is it?"

My two best friends looked at me, waiting for my answer. I wanted so much to tell them, but again, I knew they would just get worried. Besides, how would I start that conversation? There was just so much I left out from them. I couldn't even get into it.

"It's all of it," I lied. "Keon, work, and not sleeping." I laughed. "Trust, if it was something really that bad, you guys know that I would tell you." They nodded and we got to work. I hated lying to them, but right now wasn't the right time to let them in on it. One day I'll tell them.

Present:

"Jayla!" Keon called out to me. I was still in bed because it was Saturday and my day off. Usually I would be up and in the kitchen making breakfast, but I was so down. This whole mess of drama had me so depressed. What made it worse was that Darius wasn't really answering his texts. When I asked him what he was up to, all he said was that he was taking care of it. I never found out what happened when he went back to work. Did he blow up at Jamar? I didn't see any murders on the news, so at least I knew he didn't kill him. But I knew that something happened, and not knowing what it was, is what was keeping me up.

I forced myself out of bed. I looked in the mirror and saw how horrible I looked. I had bags under my eyes. I shook my head and headed to my bathroom. I took a nice warm shower, and when I got out, I felt a bit better. I got dressed in casual clothing. I walked towards the kitchen and thought about starting breakfast. When I opened my fridge full of groceries, I just shook my head. I didn't even have the strength.

"Keon!" I yelled.

"What's up sis?" he asked as he stepped out of his room.

"How about we go out for breakfast?" I suggested.

"Really?" His face scrunched up. "But you don't really go out for breakfast when we have a packed fridge."

"I know. I'm just not in the mood." I sighed.

"Are you okay?"

"I'm good," I lied. "So, do you want to go out for breakfast or not? Or maybe you're trying to volunteer to cook for us," I joked. When I said that, he grabbed his jacket and walked out the door.

"I'll wait for you by the car," he said, and I busted out laughing.

We got to the restaurant and I ordered the pancakes and sausages. Keon of course ordered like he was a pregnant woman.

"Alright." He looked over the menu. "I'll have the pancakes, eggs, sausages, hash browns, and some coffee." He handed the menu to the waitress.

"Is that all?" I laughed. "You sure you are not going to want anything more?" He playfully shook his head no.

When the food got to us, I ate a little bit. I still didn't have much of an appetite. I don't know why, but the whole time I was there, I was waiting for someone to pop up. I kept looking over my shoulder or looking towards the entrance and exits. I just was waiting for someone to pop up on me. It was like if I didn't turn my head fast enough, a gun was going to pop up on me. Who knew what else Shenice and Jamar had up their sleeves? They might have someone following me all the time. They might have someone waiting for me right outside. Was I ever going to be safe?

"Are you alright Jayla?" Keon asked as he was finishing his food.

"I'm fine." I grinned. "Why? What's up?"

"You tell me. You are barely eating your food, you not talking much, and you keep looking around like you're scared of something. What's going on?"

"Nothing."

"Stop lying to me. What is going on?"

Keon crossed his arms and was standing firm. He just waited for me to speak. I rolled my eyes.

"You remember when I got home the other night and I told you about basically almost dying?"

"Yeah. I tried to get more out of you, but you were so out of it that you never told me anything. I was going to ask you about it, but I thought it would be best to give you some space. So, what's up?"

"While I was out with Darius—" Keon cut me off by sucking teeth.

"That nigga..."

"Keon, this is not about Darius."

"Oh, it's not? You haven't noticed that all this drama in your life started after you got with this married dude? You don't think that it's more than a coincidence? You really need to be smart and cut this guy out of your life."

"Look, I know you're not a fan of Darius's—"

"What is there to be a fan of?" He cut me off again. "What has he really done that makes him a stand-up guy? What makes him worth all this aggravation?"

"I love him."

"Fuck that love bullshit. You're smarter than this Jayla, but you get stuck on stupid for that motherfucker."

"It's not about Darius. You didn't even let me finish the story."

Keon was shaking his head back and forth. He really hated Darius, and hearing this story didn't help that matter at all. This was only going to make him hate Darius more, which was why I didn't want to bring it up in the first place.

"See, this is why I didn't want to tell you."

"Why? Because I would tell you what you don't want to hear?" His eyebrow jumped up. He sighed. "Go ahead and tell me the story."

"Try not to talk shit about Darius while I do it."

"I can't tell you that I'm going to do something that I know I can't promise." He gave me a small grin. "So, what happened?"

"Well Darius and I were at a bar having a great time. He looked like he was getting way past tipsy, so I suggested that we take a walk in the park. I thought the nice night breeze would make him feel better—"

"Can we wrap this up? I don't need to be hearing that this motherfucker can't hold his liquor either." He didn't even try to pretend to like Darius, not even for two seconds.

"So"—I rolled my eyes— "we walked, and someone pulled a gun on us. They pulled the trigger, but they missed. We got in the car and drove off. But the thing is, I don't think it was a random event. I don't think we were just in the wrong place at the wrong time."

"You saying that you were set up?" His shocked face told it all.

"Yeah, I really do."

He got real still. He raised his hand up. The waitress came over to him and took out her notepad. He ordered some more coffee. I asked for some green tea. After we sipped some our drinks, he started again.

"Jayla, do you have any clue to who it is? Do you know who it is? Or are you just guessing at this point?"

"I'm not guessing at all Keon. I'm telling you that I know who it is. Remember when I told you about seeing Darius's wife Shenice, with his best friend? I think they set me up. I won't put it past Shenice."

"His wife set you up?" he asked, and I nodded my head. He chuckled and shook his head. "This shit is getting too twisted. If this is true...I don't even know what to say."

"I told Darius and—"

"Wait, what? You told Darius?"

"Of course."

"Fuck!" He cursed very loudly. Some of the other people around us stop and stared at us.

"What's wrong?" I lowered my voice, hoping that he would do the same.

"Why the fuck would you tell him?"

"Why not?"

"Because now everyone knows." His eyes opened wide.

"Meaning? I don't understand what you're trying to say.

"Now, with everyone knowing, someone is going to make a dumb and hasty decision. Everyone is on edge," he told me.

"Oh shit. I didn't think of that."

I hated when Keon was right, and now that was happening more than ever. I don't know if it was getting shot that had changed him, but now he had this certain type of insight that I was grateful for. He wasn't being his usual hotheaded mess. He was calmer and smarter. I always knew that this guy was there, but to be honest, I thought I would never see him. Keon loved the streets, and it reminded me so much of our dad that it scared me. My father died because of the streets. I didn't want the same to happen to him. I was glad that he had cooled down.

Now that he was this new guy, I could rely on him. And for that, I was so grateful.

"Look sis, you have to be careful now. You have to be smart, because everybody knows, so it's only a matter of time before something happens. And once that happens, it's only going to be more problems and more bullshit," he warned me.

Chapter 6

Darius

I sat across from Shenice at the table while the lunch that she laid out in front of me was getting cold. She was eating quietly. Our daughter was with her mother, but instead of Shenice dropping her off, it was me. I needed to be with my wife alone, and I didn't want any distractions. When I got home from work, she greeted me at the door, which was weird. She hasn't greeted me at the door in years. She claimed that she missed me, but I knew that this was all because of what happened between me and Jamar. I just walked past her that night and went straight to bed. In the morning I woke up, played with my five-year-old daughter, and then brought her to her grandmother's place.

"Are you not hungry?" Shenice asked with a fake, cheesy smile. As she looked at me, all I could think about was her fucking with Jamar.

"I don't have much of an appetite," I told her.

"Is everything okay?" she had the nerve to ask me. I bit my tongue and just shook my head. "Okay. Well I'm done." She stood up and took her plate. "I think I'm going to run some errands."

"Let me come with you." She froze when I said that. I stood up and walked past her on my way to the kitchen.

As I wrapped up the food and put it in the fridge, she finally walked into the kitchen.

"Oh honey, you don't have to come with me." She was still putting up this act.

"Oh don't you worry, it's not a problem for me." I winked at her. "I'm just going to get ready and we can go."

"No, it's okay Darius. You don't—"

"No. I'm coming with you," I flat out told her.

I waited in the car for her outside. I didn't want her to leave before me. I know she was probably inside making all types of plans with Jamar, but she wasn't going to leave or try to escape at all. When I noticed that I was outside by myself for more than two minutes, I leaned on the horn. I kept honking on the horn until she came out.

"What's wrong with you?" she asked, running out. "Are you trying to annoy the entire neighborhood?"

"What's taking you so long? You were already dressed. What is it that you had to do?"

"You're clocking me now?"

"I'm just asking you a simple question Shenice. Can't I, as your husband of over ten years, ask you this question?" I looked her right in the eye. "What were you doing?"

"I was using the bathroom. Is that okay Darius? Is that okay with you?" she snapped.

"Get in."

The whole car ride was quiet and awkward. We went to pick up some dry cleaning, bought something for our daughter, and then went grocery shopping. When we were walking to the grocery store, I saw it was next to a lingerie store. I then realized that this might just be the place where Jayla had spotted Shenice and Jamar.

"What a nice lingerie shop," I said out loud. I was hoping that she would answer, but she stayed quiet. "Don't you think so?" I asked.

"Huh?" She was pretending like she didn't hear me.

"I was talking about that lingerie shop. I just noticed it. I was wondering what you thought of it?"

"It's okay." She didn't even look at it. She started power walking.

"How about we go inside and get you something?"

She paused once again. I knew she was scared. She knew that if we went in there, there was a possibility that she might be recognized.

"We don't have that type of time." She tried to brush it off. "Let's just go and get these groceries." She tried to walk to the store, but I wasn't going to make it that easy. I was going to see how far I could push this.

"We have all the time in the world." I took her hand. "Come on. Let's just go inside there and get you something sexy." I started walking towards the lingerie store.

"No." She pulled away.

"Why not?" I crossed my arms. "I just want to get you something nice and sexy. Can't I get something nice and sexy for my wife?" I watched her fidget and move around, looking for an answer.

"I just don't want to."

"We'll just be two minutes."

"Darius, I—"

"Or how about I bring a picture of you in there and see what the sales associate suggests?"

"No!" she screamed.

People around us stopped and stared at us. When they saw that it was nothing serious, they went back to their normal activities. She was noticeably upset, but I didn't care. She was skirting around this whole issue, and I was starting to get tired of this.

"You know what? It's not that important." I dropped the issue. "Let's just go grocery shopping."

We went to the grocery store, and I just followed slowly behind her. We didn't talk to each other at all. We barely looked at each other. Had anybody else been watching us, they would have thought that we were strangers and not husband and wife. We seemed so disconnected. It was weird and awkward.

"Do we need anything else?" she mumbled to me. I just shrugged my shoulders. We went over to the cashier. I knew we must have really looked bad, because the cashier looked at us weirdly when I took my card out to pay. After we got out, I looked back over at the lingerie shop. I wanted to so badly to go inside and just have someone else confirm what Jayla saw, but seeing how Shenice reacted was all the confirmation that I needed. She looked like she was going to shit herself.

Shenice started cooking dinner, and I pretended to be into the TV show I was watching. I don't even know what it was, but I just wanted my brain to be occupied for a minute. Jayla was texting me, but I kept telling her that I would get to her when I could. I couldn't stand this secret dangling over my head. It was eating away at me to not say anything. I just kept staring at her. Who is this woman that was in my house? I've known Shenice for years, and it was like I was living with a stranger. It was like I'm not even sure what was going to happen to me next.

"Dinner," she said flatly while she put my plate down. Instead of sitting opposite of me, she sat next to me. She made grilled chicken, salad, french fries, and Spanish rice. It all smelled great, but the way she smacked it on the table, it pissed me off. But I let all of that go and managed to thank her anyway. It was delicious, and I somehow got myself to eat two or three spoonfuls. I glanced over at Shenice, and she was barely eating as well. This whole thing was just hanging over our heads.

"What the fuck are we doing?" I muttered under my breath.

"What did you say? I can't hear you."

"What the fuck are we doing?!" I shouted and pounded my fist against the table. She jumped up and looked at me.

"What are you talking about? We're eating dinner." Her voice was still cold and flat, like it was before. Despite the fact that she jumped up earlier, she was still the same.

"I'm not talking about fucking dinner, Shenice, and you know that. You know what I'm talking about."

"No, I honestly don't."

"Honestly?" Hearing that word made me mad. "Did you fucking bring up honesty?"

"Yes I did," she tried to say casually. "Maybe we should both be honest." She gave me a side look.

That was when I knew that she was purposely playing with me. I got even angrier.

"I know the truth," I told her.

"Do you?"

"Yes." I pushed the plate away.

"And what truth is this Darius?"

"I am not in the mood for some games, Shenice."

"You're not?" She was still using that playful tone, and it was making me angrier. "Hmmm."

"What the fuck is that supposed to mean?"

"Nothing." She was starting to actually eat now.

I sat back in my chair and just watched her. She was getting a kick out of this; I knew it. To her, she was now watching me suffer. Was this payback? Was this her way of getting revenge on me? I know I'm not innocent in all of this, but did that mean that I deserved to die? Did this mean that I brought on the fact that she and my best friend got together? I still wanted to know when did this start. That was what was pissing me off too. She was still having sex with me. So was she having sex with me and Jamar at the same time? Did she fuck him in our house?

On our bed? Did she bring him around while my daughter was here?

"Tell me the truth Shenice," I demanded.

"The truth about what?"

"Stop fucking playing with me. You know what I'm talking about. Just tell me the truth and we can go from there. But stop playing these fucking games."

"Games? What games?" She was still trying to play me, and it was taking everything in me to not start yelling. I took a deep breath and kept my cool.

"When did it start?"

"When did what start?"

"Come on Shenice, let's not play stupid. We both know what I'm talking about, and we both want to talk about it."

"What are you talking about Darius?" She turned to look at me. "Are you asking me to be honest about something?"

"Yes."

"So you want me to tell the truth about something?"

"Yes."

"So, ask me."

The tension in the room got thicker as we both remained silent. All you could hear was that damn grandfather clock ticking in the background. It's never been this quiet in this house. With a little one, this house was usually filled with laughter, crying, talking, and love. But now, as I sat next to my wife, it was just filled with...hate. Maybe hate was a strong word, but whatever this feeling was that was in the air, it wasn't love. It was the opposite of love.

She looked at me, expecting me to say something, and I was ready to, but a part of me knew that once I asked Shenice the question, I couldn't turn back. As much as I was ready for the truth, was I ready to hear it from her? Was I ready to hear it from the same lips that years ago had told me "I do"? The same lips that kissed me goodnight, the same lips that said they loved me, were now turning against me. What was going on?

"Shenice, what's going on?"

"I don't know Darius, since you refuse to ask me. What is going on?"

"What is going on with you? What have you been up to lately?"

"I've been doing what I've always been doing. If you would be more specific, I'm sure I'll be able to answer your question, dear." She gave me a condescending smile. "You keep talking about me being more honest, yet you won't ask me what it is that you need to know. It seems like, if anything, you're the one with something to hide." She picked at her food again. "So, what is it that you want to know?"

"What's going on with you and Jamar?'

She dropped her fork. It was quiet again, and that damn clock kept ticking away. I pushed my chair away from the dining room table and waited for her answer. She was still not saying a word, but I was looking at her face. I wanted to see if I could read anything. Was she going to give it up like she did in the parking lot of the grocery store? When I mentioned the lingerie shop, her face had told it all, so I was just waiting for some sort of clue to show on her face. Maybe something would pop up on her face and she would just finally tell it all.

"What about Jamar?" She leaned back in her chair. "What are you asking, Darius?"

"Is there something going on with you and Jamar?" I asked. "Let me know."

"Why are you asking that?"

"Answer the question."

"Answer mine first," she spat back. "Why are you asking that question?"

"You're really going to prolong this huh?" I chuckled. I looked around at the table and noticed that her phone wasn't there. She was wearing this sleeveless dress that had no pockets. "Where is your phone?"

That was when her face changed. Now I knew that something for sure was going on between her and Jamar. Jayla was right, and Shenice's face just told me that.

"Where is your phone?" I asked while I stood up. I started to make my way to the bedroom. She always kept her phone charged on the nightstand. It was a habit of hers that she had ever since she used to be in real estate. She was the one that taught me that a phone had to be close to 100 percent at all times.

"You never know when a client will call you, and the last thing you need is for your phone to be dead. Or worse, your phone dies in the middle of an important conversation. Make sure your phone is always plugged in and charged up," she'd told me back in the day. I knew that more than likely her phone was in the bedroom charging.

"Where are you going?" She got up behind me.

"Where do you think I'm going?" I snapped back with my head slightly over my shoulder. "I'm going to get your phone."

"Don't you touch my phone."

"Why? You have something to hide?" I stopped a foot away from our bedroom. "What's on your phone that I can't see?"

"I have nothing to hide."

"Then I'm going to go get your phone." I started walking to the bedroom again, but she moved past me and ran into the bedroom.

Shenice grabbed her phone and put it in her bra.

"Give me your phone Shenice." I held out my hand, waiting for her to drop it in my palm.

"No." She crossed her arms.

"Why not?" With a crooked smile on my face, I continued. "What's on your phone that I can't see? Is there something you're hiding from me? Something from Jamar? Maybe some phone calls? Or maybe some text messages that you don't want me to see?"

"Nothing like that; I just think that this is an invasion of privacy."

"I'm sure you do think that, but then again, you said that you had nothing to hide. So, I thought that it wouldn't be a problem if I looked through your phone."

"You really want my phone?"

"Yes." I nodded my head. "I really do."

"Cool. I'll give you mine if you give me yours." She crossed her arms.

I suddenly got stiff. I thought about the last time I texted or called Jayla. I would usually make sure to delete it right after just in case Shenice ever got a hold of my phone, but lately I've been slipping on that. More times than not, I would forget that I had pictures from Jayla, or messages from her, or even phone calls. I was forgetting, and it was even more of a problem. I knew that if I handed her my phone, she'd find pictures of Jayla...along with other things.

"This is childish." I shook my head. "All I'm asking you is for you to tell me the truth."

"And all I'm asking is for you to give me what you want from me. How about this, Darius? How about any question you ask me, I can turn around and ask you?" Her nose flared as she looked me up and down. "So? You ready?" she went on.

"What do you mean?"

"Oh, now look who is playing stupid?" She laughed, and I gritted my teeth. "Now look who is ducking and dodging questions."

"Now we going to go back and forth?"

"Why not? Just like you want answers, maybe I want some answers too."

"So we going to go for tit for tat?'

I started walking away. This conversation was not going the way I had planned. She was now turning this whole thing into something spiteful. She was just going to throw things in my face now. Now she was going to avoid the whole thing by being petty, and that was not going to help the situation. If she was going to do this, it was not going to be a good situation at all. It was just going to end up being a screaming match with nothing being solved. I was not going to be sucked into that.

"Where are you going?" She was right behind me. "I thought you wanted to know the truth, but as soon as I turned it around on you, you're not interested. How about we both go back and forth and get everything out?"

"I'm not going to be pulled into an argument with you, Shenice," I told her, but she wasn't going to give up that easy. She was still right behind me.

"No, let's do it. You wanted to go, let's fucking go. You wanted to talk, let's fucking talk. I will tell you everything that you want to know, but only after you go first."

"Not now Shenice."

"What? What is it?" she snapped. "Now you change your mind because maybe your secrets will come out?"

"Secrets?" I screwed up my face.

"Yes. Maybe you got some secrets too?"

I was about to leave, but then I heard the last word that she said. I don't even think she realized it. Her face was still mad, so I knew that she didn't catch it either.

"You just said too," I pointed it out.

"What?"

"You said that maybe I had secrets too, which means that you have secrets." When I said this, her face dropped. "So like I've been saying all fucking day, do you have something to tell me?"

She didn't bother to answer. She went to the kitchen and started to wash the dishes. I just followed her and waited for her to say something, but she didn't. She was really going to act like I hadn't caught her in a corner. She rinsed both of the dishes and set them on the rack. She dried her hands and walked past me. She then sat down on the couch and turned on the TV.

"Are you fucking serious!" I screamed. "Shenice!" She calmly turned to look at me. "Talk to me! Fucking talking to me!"

"What is it that you want to know?!" she yelled. "What is it Darius?"

"Are you fucking Jamar?!" She looked away. "Look at me when I'm fucking talking to you."

"Watch your tone."

"Answer me." I brought my voice down. "Have you been fucking Jamar?"

"Are you really going to ask me that?"

"And you're still ducking and dodging this question." I laughed. "You're still going to pretend that I'm not asking you..." I drifted off. I was getting so mad that I couldn't even speak. "What the fuck?" I whispered.

Shenice just rolled her eyes and shrugged her shoulders. She went back to watching TV. She was just so cold and distant. She was not only resembling a stranger, but she was like this ice queen. Nothing I said to her was really getting through. She was just flipping everything back to me. It seemed as if she was just going to avoid the truth by arguing with me. Fuck it; I wanted answers.

"Have you been cheating on me by sleeping with my best friend Jamar?"

"Are you asking me if I've been faithful?"

"Shenice..." I closed my eyes, trying to reach for some patience. "Please, I am trying my best to not start yelling again."

"So, what is it?" She turned off the TV. "What is it that you want to know?"

"Are you...fucking...Jamar?"

"Are you fucking someone else?" She threw the question back at me. "Are you being honest with me? Are you being unfaithful?" She stood up and crossed her arms. "You answer these questions and I'll answer yours."

Epilogue

Darius

The conversation got really loud quickly. She kept playing the same game, and it was exhausting. We just kept going back and forth. One minute I was trying to get her to tell the truth, and the other minute she was trying to get me to confess about Jayla. It was like she knew about her, but she wouldn't say it. She was waiting for me to confess.

"So what about you?" she threw back at me like she had been doing this whole time. "Are you sleeping with someone else? Are you fucking around?" She rolled her neck. "Because as much as you want me to be honest, I want you to be honest too. I know that you've cheated before—"

"I thought we got past it."

"Oh I got past those times. I've gotten over those times that I've caught you cheatin' in the past."

"Then why are you bringing it up?"

"Because maybe you are trying to make me feel guilty for something you did. Maybe you are doing wrong but you want to put that all on me."

"I just want to know the truth."

"I want to know the truth too."

I took another deep breath. I headed for the fridge and grabbed a beer. I broke off the cap by slamming it against counter. I chugged it and took it to the head. I needed to calm down. My nerves were everywhere and I was really upset and I didn't want to start yelling again. I never liked raising my voice. I've always liked being chill, but this was a situation that was going to bring out the worst in me. Slowly but surely, I was getting more and more aggravated.

I sat on the chair. I laid my head on the table just to get a few seconds to myself. I just needed to clear my head.

"Darius..." But it looked like Shenice was not going to let that happen.

"What is it Shenice?"

"Are we going to talk?" She pulled a chair out next to me.

"Like really talk? Or are we going to bullshit for another few hours?"

"It depends," she said wickedly, and I shot her an evil look.

"Depends on what? Depends on if you want to waste more of my fucking time?" I shot my head up. "Or does it depend on whether or not you're really fucking my friend?"

I got up and walked away, but I came back.

"You know how much Jamar means to me. You know that I think of him as my brother. He is more than just a good friend of mine; he's fucking family to me. So to think that you will go and do that, it really fucks me up."

"But why are you asking me about me and Jamar?"

"What?" I was confused.

"Like, where did this accusation come from? You've never come at me like this before," she told me. "You've never ever accused me of something like this."

"So…" I didn't get it. "What are you getting at?"

"Who told you this ridiculous story of something going on between me and Jamar?"

And there once again was her asking me about Jayla. She knew that if I mentioned how I knew about her and Jamar, I would have to bring up Jayla.

"Does it matter?" I asked. "Does it really matter where I got this story from? Does it really matter? All that matters is the truth."

"You know what? You are so right about that. All that matters is the truth. So how about you tell me the truth?"

"What do you want to know?"

"Where is this coming from all of a sudden? Where is this coming from? Did somebody tell you something?" she said out of nowhere. "Did someone just plant some crazy ideas in your head?'

I wanted to get another drink, but I didn't want to cloud my mind. Last thing I needed was to get drunk and say some stuff that I would regret.

"Who cares?" I threw back at her. "Are you sleeping with Jamar?"

"Are you sleeping with someone else?"

"Answer the question."

"You answer the fucking question." Her eyes were cold again. "We've been married for ten years, and the last few years have been some bullshit."

"Oh yeah?"

"Yes Darius. Don't pretend that you have been the best husband. You've lied and cheated. You've hid many things from me, and now you want to come and talk about honesty. Do you really want to talk about honesty Darius? Honestly, you've treated me like shit."

"Is this your way of justifying what you've done? Are you saying these things so that you won't feel so guilty for fucking my friend?"

She swallowed hard. She began to open her mouth to say something, but she stopped herself. She bit her bottom lip. We just stood there staring at each other, not saying a word. I was waiting for her to say something, and I was sure she was waiting for me to say something. I just couldn't take it anymore.

"If you want me to apologize to you for all that I've done, I'll do it. Even though I've said this to you before, I'm sorry for all that I've done Shenice. I know that it really hurt you, and that was never my intention. I can't tell you enough how sorry I am, because I'm starting to see that there is nothing I can do to make up for it. But regardless of anything, I am sorry. But do not take what I did in the past and do this to me, to our family."

Then she started to laugh. She threw her head back and laughed at me. I just spilled my guts and she just threw that back in my face. I got to a place where I was really vulnerable, and now she was making me regret it.

"Are you being serious?" She was still laughing. "Are you really going to use our daughter against me? What? Did you think by bringing her up that you were going to make some sort of confession to something? You know, I thought you were a piece of shit before, but now...I know for sure that you are a piece of shit. And to use our daughter—"

"I didn't do that. I was just letting you know how sorry I was. I didn't mean for it to—"

"Oh, you never fucking mean for shit. You didn't mean to cheat on me. You didn't mean to break our vows. You didn't mean to be a fuckboy. You didn't mean. You never fucking mean to do shit, but you always do. And then you never stop doing the bullshit."

"What are you saying?"

"I know for a fact that you're still fucking around. So stop trying to sell me this whole honesty bit when you're not being honest yourself."

She brought up the whole Jayla thing, and I hated when she did. She was right, but I couldn't let her know that.

"Why do you keep avoiding the question?" I confronted her on it. "Do you realize that you have yet to give me a straight answer to my question?"

"Well maybe because you spent a whole lot of time pussyfooting around the question."

"Then let me ask you once again, flat out. Have you been fucking around?"

"Have you?"

"And we're still going to do this?" I shook my head. "We're still going to be going back and forth." When I saw her shrug her shoulders, I had enough. I walked to the front door and I grabbed my keys.

"Where are you going?" she asked.

"Out."

"To your whore?" She laughed wickedly.

"Whatever Shenice." I opened the door. "Just promise me that you'll wait ten minutes before calling Jamar over here to fuck you senseless." I slammed the door behind me. I got in my car, started the engine, and pulled out. I looked in my rearview mirror and saw Shenice coming out with her arms crossed. There was only one thing I wanted to do right now.

"Hey babe!" Jayla's bright and bubbly voice brought a smile to my face. The second I heard her voice, all the stress I had just washed away from me. She is such a relief to come to. I just needed to see her, because she is just the sunshine after the storm.

"What's up? Would you mind if I came over to see you?"

"Of course not." I could sense her smile from here. "Is everything okay? I haven't heard from you really. I mean there were a few short calls and some text messages, but I don't really know what's going through your head. I know that I dropped a huge bomb on you. I just want to know if you're okay."

"To tell you the truth, I don't know if I could ever be okay with Jamar and Shenice. The thought of them two together just makes me so sick." I shook my head. "But enough about that. I just want to see you."

"And talk about our future?" she asked carefully. I smiled at that.

"And talk about our future," I confirmed. "We have a lot to talk about Jayla. I just..." I sighed. "I just can't wait to see you."

"I can't wait to see you too." Her tone and voice was so positive. She was so opposite of Shenice.

"And what about Keon? I know I'm not his favorite person."

"Don't you worry about Keon. I'll talk to him."

"Love you Jayla. You don't even know how much I do."

"I love you too Darius."

"I'll see you later."

"I'll be ready when you get here."

I was driving top speed to get to Jayla's condo. I just needed to be around her positive energy. Everything I've been through with Shenice was just so draining. I don't know how we got to where we are, but it's so exhausting. Every day was a new fight or a new battle with her. On the good days with Shenice, it was good, but on the bad days? The bad days were hell. It was just utter chaos. It wasn't a healthy marriage, and it hasn't been for quite some time.

Flashback:

One of the first women I cheated with was this young woman who was working for my firm. It was just brand new and it was so stressful. I was hiring people, figuring out how to run the business, and just trying to be a boss. At the same time, I was a newlywed husband. Shenice and I then were so obsessed with each other. Then one day she just changed. I didn't know what it was, or maybe I didn't know what I did, but it wasn't the same. She started to be vindictive and mean. So one day when she had a bad attitude, I went to the office to escape.

I was going to put everything into my work, but when I got there, Vanessa, the new worker, was there.

Vanessa was gorgeous and stacked. She reminded me of a curvier Lisa Bonet. She had those beautiful eyes that you could get lost in. She also had this soft and sultry voice. When she spoke, she sounded like sex. Sometimes I would get hard just hearing her speak. So when I saw her in the office sitting by herself, I was drawn to her.

"I hope you don't mind." She quickly came up with an excuse. "I am just looking at new listings. I am so excited because I got my license. I just couldn't wait to get started."

"How did you get the key?"

"I asked the janitor if I could stay while he cleaned up. He finished, so I promised to lock up in about ten minutes."

"How long ago was that?"

"About an hour ago." She gave me a slick smile. "I'm sorry," she apologized again.

One thing led to another and then we were just having sex. I was not clear on who made the first move, but I do remember us just leaning into a kiss. I didn't stop at that. Once I started sleeping with her, it was kind of hard to stop. Any time I went home to Shenice and she was bitching about something, I would just go escape to the office and screw Vanessa.

One night, Vanessa invited me over to her place. She lived in this small studio apartment. It was tiny, but it was so neat. As soon as you stepped in, you just knew a woman lived there. She surprised me at the door, wearing lingerie and heels. Her beautiful and curvy bottle was like a magnet. I wrapped my arms around that waist and pulled her in for a kiss. She went straight for my dick. She didn't wait or play around. Maybe that was another reason why I was so addicted to her. She just went straight for what she wanted.

"Take this off." She was pulling my pants down. She pulled out my rock-hard dick and shoved it into her mouth. She was all over the place. One second she was giving me head and the next she was bending herself completely over. She would push me onto the floor and climb on top of me. She would roll her hips like a professional.

"Are you a dancer?" I asked her once we'd finished having sex.

"Not for money," she teased, biting on her tongue. "But I do take pole dancing classes."

"You do?"

"Yes. It was something I did after I lost a lot of weight. I wanted to learn how to move my new body and I wanted to feel sexy."

"So you can work a pole?"

"Yup. I can do splits in the air and all that."

"You just got sexier." I kissed her nose.

"Closer and closer to wifey material," she mentioned, and when she saw my face change, she just shook her head. "I was kidding."

"Okay." I brushed it off, but I shouldn't have.

I should have taken that conversation more seriously. I just ignored it, but that conversation was a hint of what was to come. Right around that time, Vanessa started making more jokes like that. She would always say that she should be my wife, or she would ask me to stay the night. I had to dance around those questions, but it didn't stop her. She wanted more and more. She then made a request that stopped me cold.

Vanessa had been begging me for some time to take a vacation with her. I thought she was crazy, because she knew I was married. She knew about Shenice, but now she didn't care. In the beginning of the relationship, she told me that she was fine with her position. She used to tell me that she loved being a girl on the side because she got to have all the fun. She said that it was okay for her, but as time went on, she wanted to be more than that.

As we went on, she didn't want to be my mistress anymore. She started asking me flat out to make her my girlfriend. She was begging me to take her on a vacation so that we could go to a place where no one knew us. She wanted to be able to hold my hand and for us to act like a couple in public, but I wasn't having that. I tried to take some time away from her. I was hoping that if I saw her less, she wouldn't want me as much. Or maybe if I saw her less, she would get the hint and back off. I tried to concentrate back on my wife, but Vanessa wasn't having that. As soon as she saw me pulling away, she started to show her true colors.

It started out with text messages. She started saying that she wasn't going to be pushed to the side. I ignored it at first, but when she called the house phone, I panicked.

"Hello?" I picked up the phone.

"Aren't you lucky?" Vanessa's voice made me freeze. "I was really hoping to get your wife."

"Are you crazy?"

"Now why do I have to be crazy? You're the one who fucks me and then act like you can throw me away like trash. I am a person Darius, and you will treat me like a person."

"I'm sorry."

"Don't do that. Don't give me a half-ass apology because you're afraid your world is going to crumble. Did you really think you could have the both of us? You're so selfish that you probably did." I didn't say anything, because Shenice was just in the other room and I didn't want her to hear. "Are you there?"

"Yes, I'm here."

"Good, because..."

She then went on a rant about how much she hated me. I was a user and the sex wasn't even that great. She told me of how she faked it and was surprise that I could stay hard. She didn't hold back, and I barely said anything. I was thinking that if I let her get it all out, maybe she would back down.

"And I can do better than you," she finally finished. "Okay?"

"I'm sorry you feel like that."

"Feel like that?" She chuckled. "Is your wife around? How about you pass her the phone so I can tell her how I feel? Then maybe she can turn around and tell me how she feels."

"That's not necessary."

"How about I see what is necessary?" She ended the call.

She kept calling the house and hanging up when it was me. I made sure to always pick up the phone when I was home. On the days I wasn't home, I would turn the ringer off. Then on some other days, I would just disconnect the phone. When Shenice complained about the phone not working, I convinced her that we had to change the number. She agreed and we made it private. After that, things were running smoothly. Vanessa left the job to work at another real estate firm and my marriage was working well.

The doorbell rang one night, and Shenice ran to go get it. I didn't think nothing of it and assumed that she had done some online shopping and that it was a package coming in. After ten minutes of her being at the door, I got suspicious.

"Shenice, who is it?" She didn't say anything, and it was still quiet. "Shenice?" I listened closely and heard whispering. I got up, and when I saw Vanessa at my doorway, my heart dropped. Everything from there went into slow motion. Vanessa was looking real sorry as she told my wife of all the sex we'd had. Before I could even think of denying it, she showed my wife a video clip of us together. I was stupid for ever letting her do it, and now it was being used against me.

The look on Shenice's face after Vanessa finished telling her almost killed me. She just looked at me like she didn't know who I was. She left me for about a month. During that whole month, I begged and pleaded with her to take me back. We'd only been married for a year, and I didn't want to give up on us. It looked like she'd just given up on us and that she didn't want to deal with me anymore. I tried and tried.

Finally, I got through to her, and she said that the only way that she'd get back with me was if we went to some counseling. I agreed to it. We went to some church and sat with a bishop. He heard our stories and he just beat into me that it was my fault. I had accepted that, but I guess I was expecting for him to ask Shenice if she felt she had any part of it. I thought he would ask me why I didn't turn to my wife while I was dealing with everything by myself, but it almost felt like him and Shenice were in some sort of agreement. I could never prove it, but that was what it had felt like.

The counseling seemed to work and everything got a bit smoother. But then it happened again. I cheated again. Once I cheated once, it got easier and easier to do. It wasn't such a heartbreak anymore. I would just choose females who would never get back to Shenice. I think maybe that was why I'm so hurt by the whole Jamar thing. It was not that she cheated, but that she did it with him. She could have done that with anybody else, but she chose him because she knew it would kill me. If she slept with some random guy, I would feel some pain, but her with Jamar?

Knowing that she and Jamar slept together was making me slowly die inside. And now my marriage was at such a negative place that I don't see no way out of this. I don't see any way of us coming back to a good place. I don't see us being that happily married couple that we used to be. That dream is dead and buried.

Present:

I parked in the parking lot of Jayla's condo. I leaned my head against the steering wheel. I took in a deep breath. I could not let what was going on with my wife and Jamar affect what was going on between me and Jayla. The whole point of me leaving Shenice at the house was to leave all that negativity behind. Once I get out of this car, I will just take on a new day and a new attitude. From now on, it was going to be nothing but positive vibes.

Turning off the ignition, I got out of the car. I locked it and then put the car alarm on. I started walking towards the steps until I heard the chirp. I looked farther down the parking lot and saw that someone was there. I wasn't going to pay them much attention, but the way they were moving and how they were acting was very strange. Seeing how much drama I've been through, I was especially going to be aware of my surroundings. This person was walking weird. I just shrugged it off and kept heading to the staircase. But then the closer I got to the stairs, the closer the person got to me. Once they were right in front of me, I knew I was fucked.

Jayla

I couldn't wait for Darius to get here. Now that he knew about Jamar and Shenice, everything was a bit better. I didn't have this guilt hanging over my head. It was hard to let him know, but after the shooting, it would be wrong to keep it to myself.

I got out a bottle of wine and two glasses. I was going to whip something up to eat, but I was too nervous to cook. I just kept wondering what it was that he was going to tell me. Was he going to tell me that he served her the divorce papers? Was he going to tell me that she admitted to everything? Did Jamar admit to anything? As messy as it is, wouldn't that be the perfect scenario. If Jamar and Shenice got to be together, then me and Darius could definitely be together much easier. We won't have to worry about her being spiteful during the divorce because she would already have someone. She might just sign the papers, let them split everything equally, and just live happily with Jamar. If only this could come true.

Pacing back and forth around the condo, I was getting more and more anxious. I wanted to call Darius again, but I didn't want to bug him. If he said he was going to come over, I had to believe that was going to be the case. He was probably getting something for us to eat or maybe just clearing his head before he got here. It used to be that Darius would say he was coming over and would get here as fast as he could. Maybe all that nonsense at home has got him on some sort of new schedule. Maybe he just needed a breather or two., but whatever it is, once he gets here, we will finally talk about our future.

I've been waiting for this talk for so long. I have to admit that Darius had been putting it off, but that didn't matter now. It was all in the past. Now I just had to be happy that it was all coming together. Darius was going to leave Shenice, he and I were going to be together, and I'll finally have my one big happy family. It couldn't get any better than this.

I didn't want to push things, but I wondered how long before Darius and I get married and have kids. I didn't want to rush anything, because I knew that divorces could get dirty, but I just couldn't help but to think of what my life was going to be like with

Darius. We could have a little boy who would look just like him, or maybe a girl who could be my mini twin. We would get this big huge house with an enormous front yard. The house would have a lot of bedrooms so that Keon and my baby sister could stay over whenever they wanted. Once Keon saw all of this, he would have to eat his words about all that he's been saying about Darius. Once we had this, Keon would get on board and everything would be perfect

The loud gunshots brought me to the floor. It was followed by the sound of glass shattering. It was so loud that I knew it had to be close. It sounded like it came from right outside. I didn't live in a bad neighborhood, so it was not only scary to hear it, but also weird. I crawled on the floor. I was so frightened that I didn't want to get up. Was it the person that tried to kill me before? Was he coming back to finish the job? I don't know, but I wasn't going to give him the chance to kill me. I went by the door and made sure that the door was locked. I crawled to the bedroom window and looked out through my blinds. I had to be careful. I didn't want the person who was doing the shooting to see me looking. If they saw me looking, they would definitely come kick the door in and kill me. They do not like any witnesses.

If there is one thing I learned from growing up in the hood, it was how to keep to yourself. If you were going to look into something, you better make damn sure that no one saw you looking. Usually I would mind my business, but since the gunshots were so close, I just had to go see.

When I looked through the blinds, my palms were sweaty and my heart was racing. I was so scared. I just thought that the second I looked out, the shooter was going to see me, bring up the gun, and just start shooting. I looked, and what I saw made my heart drop. I recognized something. I saw Darius's car in the parking lot. I didn't know that he was here already. How long had he been here? Oh shit. The gunshots. What happened to Darius?

I scanned the parking lot, and I saw that his car window was shattered. I kept looking, and my heart felt heavy again. Oh my God! Something happened to Darius.

~~~

**Find out what happens next
in the final installment of His Dirty Secret
Book 6! Available Now!**

His Dirty Secret 6:

Tensions run high as the two lovers, Jayla and Darius, are now facing the consequences of their lustful affair.

Find out what happens next in the final installment of His Dirty Secret! Get Your Copy Today!

CPSIA information can be obtained at www.ICGtesting.com
Printed in the USA
LVOW10s1452070616

491590LV00014B/628/P